The world is a colourful place.

Yellow,

YOU

Stephen Michael King

■ SCHOLASTIC

First published in 2010 by Scholastic Australia
This edition first published in 2011 by Scholastic Children's Books
Euston House, 24 Eversholt Street
London NW1 1DB
a division of Scholastic Ltd
www.scholastic.co.uk

London ~ New York ~ Toronto ~ Sydney ~ Auckland
Mexico City ~ New Delhi ~ Hong Kong

Text and Illustrations copyright © 2010 Stephen Michael King

ISBN 978 1407 12449 0

All rights reserved
Printed in Singapore

1 3 5 7 9 10 8 6 4 2

The moral rights of Stephen Michael King have been asserted.

Papers used by Scholastic Children's Books are made from wood
grown in sustainable forests.

red,

blue,

all colours.

Coloured with big things,

small things,

all sorts of things.

But the most colourful part of my world is . . .

you.

ting

The world is a musical place,

with high notes

and low notes,

all the notes in between.

Thump

Thoomp!

But the most musical part of my world is . . .

you.

The world is an exciting place,

with ups,

downs,

arounds and arounds,

and far-far-aways.

But the most exciting place in my world

is with . . .

you.